Chippy's
favorite toys

Published in the United States by Grolier Enterprises, Inc.,
Danbury, Connecticut 06816.

Copyright © 1984 Victoria House Publishing Limited

Characters Copyright © 1984 Tony Hutchings

Designed by Victoria House Publishing Limited, Paulton, Bristol BS18 5LQ.

Printed in Yugoslavia

Jane Carruth   illustrated by Tony Hutchings

Chippy's favorite toys

GROLIER ENTERPRISES INC.
Danbury, Connecticut 06816

Chippy loved to help Daddy in the yard. Daddy was very busy making and fixing things and today, Chippy was helping him fix the fence. "I'm glad we're almost finished," Chippy said, as he picked up the last piece of wood. "Susan is coming over to play soon. I want to show her the mobile we made and all those wonderful boxes Mommy gave me."

"It won't take long now," Daddy said. "When we have this board straight you can hand me the nails."
"Can I hammer one in?" Chippy asked.
"Sure," said Daddy. "You're old enough now to learn how to use tools properly. Here, take the hammer."
Chippy was pleased.

What was keeping Susan? Where could she be? thought
Chippy. "You're late!" he said, when she finally arrived.
"I expected you ages ago."
"I know," said Susan, hardly stopping long enough to say,
"I'm sorry, but I can't stay. I'm going to Milton's house to
play. He has some really fantastic toys . . ."
"I don't want to hear about him or his toys!" Chippy
shouted.

And not wanting Susan to see his disappointment, he
turned suddenly and rushed into the house.
"Where is Susan?" Mommy asked, as he burst into the
kitchen. "I've baked her favorite cake."
"She isn't coming," Chippy said miserably. "She has gone
to Milton's house to play instead."
"I met Milton's mother in the market yesterday!" Mommy
said. "I thought of calling on her today!"

When Mommy saw how sad Chippy looked, she said,
"Let's go together to Milton's house right now. I'd like to
visit with his mother."
Chippy felt shy when he first arrived at Milton's. But Susan
was there and Milton, in his new playsuit, was very happy
to show Chippy his beautiful toys.

Chippy's shyness disappeared quickly when Milton showed
him how to move the vans and trucks by remote control.
"You are *so* lucky!" he cried, his eyes shining.
"I suppose so," Milton said, rather bored. "Daddy brings lots
of new toys from his office. They make toys there, you know.
The panda and the rocking horse are my newest toys."

"Could I ride on the rocking horse?" Chippy asked. "I won't go too fast, I promise."

"Sure you can," Milton said. "Hop on. I'll help Susan with the jigsaw puzzle."

Chippy climbed on to the big, handsome rocking horse with great excitement.

"Watch me! Watch me!" he shouted happily, at the top of his voice. "I'm a cowboy."

"Or a prince!" Susan shouted back.

Soon it was time to leave. Chippy talked about Milton's toys all the way home. "You can play with your own toys," Mommy told him as soon as they were in their house. "And maybe we'll have time to go to the library before bedtime." But Chippy didn't want to play with his own toys, and he didn't want to go to the library. He was *so* quiet that Mommy thought he must be sick. It wasn't like Chippy to be so silent.

When Chippy had brushed his teeth and was ready for bed, Mommy asked him if he would like to tell her what was bothering him.

"You didn't want to play with any of your toys," she said gently. "Not even your beautiful engine."

"It doesn't have remote control!" Chippy burst out tearfully. "My toys aren't as nice as Milton's, and Susan will never want to come and play here again!"

Chippy fell asleep thinking about Milton's toys. Then, he wasn't little Chippy any longer but a brave, handsome young prince, trotting through toyland on his gallant horse. Suddenly, in the distance, the prince saw a huge crane carrying off his favorite engine. Digging his heels into his prancing steed, the prince set off at a gallop to rescue the engine.

Faster and faster he galloped. Would he be too late? "I'm coming!" he shouted. "I'm coming!"

Suddenly Chippy was lying on the floor, wide awake. He
had fallen out of bed! "Mommy! Mommy!" he cried. He
wasn't a prince in a plumed hat and dashing cloak anymore.
He was just plain, old Chippy in his plain, old striped
pajamas. Mommy rushed into his room as soon as she
heard Chippy fall.

She gave Chippy a big hug as she picked him up. "You
were just having a bad dream," she said.
"I was on a horse," Chippy whispered, "riding to rescue my
engine from a huge crane."
"Well, you couldn't let anything happen to your engine,"
Mommy said, "even if it *doesn't* have remote control!"

On Saturday Chippy found Mommy busy at her sewing machine.

"What are you making?" he asked.

"It's a surprise," Mommy said, with a twinkle in her eye. Chippy laughed. "May I have some of this blue cloth that's on the floor? I want to use it for the fort I'm going to make with the boxes."

"Yes," said Mommy, secretly pleased that Chippy seemed happy to play with his toys again. "Maybe Susan will come to play with you later."

"I don't think so," said Chippy, "not when she can go to Milton's house and play with *his* toys."

But Chippy was wrong. He was busy building a high tower
with his boxes when in came Susan and Milton.
"We've brought some toy soldiers for your fort," Susan
said. "Milton wanted to see it."
"And your beautiful wooden engine," Milton said.
"It doesn't work by remote control," Chippy heard himself
saying.

"That doesn't matter!" Milton exclaimed. And then he was playing with the engine, loading it up with bricks.

When Mommy came in with some juice, she could see how much they were enjoying themselves. And when, at last, Susan said it was time to go, Milton said, "Can we come again, Chippy? This has been fun!"

"Of course," said Chippy eagerly. "Come any time."

Later that day, Chippy found that Mommy's surprise was a handsome blue playsuit. He put it on right away. Then he went to help Daddy.

Daddy was cutting out a tunnel from one of the boxes and Chippy made a path of blocks leading to the entrance.

"I'm afraid it won't be as nice as anything Milton has," Daddy said.

"Oh yes, it will!" Chippy said loudly. "Milton has terrific toys but this is great too. It is just the right size for my engine and trucks."

"That was the idea!" said Daddy, smiling.

And Chippy gave Daddy a great, big, happy smile in return.